# Sparkles of Joy

Written By

**Aditi W.Singh**

Drawings by

**Illustrations Hub**

 *A Children's Book that Celebrates Diversity and Inclusion*

Empowerment Series
Growth Mindset for Global Citizens

https://raisingworldchildren.com/

**Paperback ISBN - 978-1-7335649-4-6**
**Hardcover ISBN - 978-1-7335649-5-3**
Library of Congress Control Number -2020922027
Raising World Children LLC
Glen Allen, Virginia

*" Diversity is inviting someone to the party.*
*Inclusion is asking them to dance. "*

*- Verna Myers*

1

Riya loves planning celebrations with her ma.
She has invited her neighborhood friends for
a festive playdate.

Ella and Dev come with gifts. They admire the
Rangoli in front of the door. Warren arrives with
their new neighbor, Caleb.

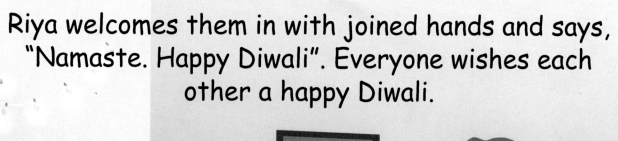

Riya welcomes them in with joined hands and says,
"Namaste. Happy Diwali". Everyone wishes each
other a happy Diwali.

"Have you settled into your new home?" Ella asks Caleb.

He nods, too shy to speak.

"Great!", she turns to Riya. "Everything looks so amazing!"

"Isn't Diwali called the Festival of Lights?"
Warren wonders.

Dev beams, "That's because homes twinkle with holiday lights and diyas. It is a celebration of good winning over evil." He punches the air with glee.

Riya asks everyone, "Would you like to try on the traditional clothes and accessories Ma set aside?" They all say yes and dress up, feeling very fancy.

Ma brings wheat flour dough. She shows them how to make diyas by shaping small balls of it into bowls with a flat bottom. Everyone enjoys molding the dough and pinching it where they will need to add the wick.

Ma takes the diyas away to bake and gives them diyas she prebaked, to design. With paint and glitter, the diyas sparkle.

After crafting, everyone munches on delicious Indian snacks of gujiyas, pedas, chiwda and chakli.

Ella passes more sweets to Caleb.

"These are so yummy. All this reminds me of Christmas. We bake and decorate our own ornaments from salt dough and my house sparkles just like this."

"Don't forget about the cards we make and exchange with friends and family," prompts Warren. "Do you like making cards, Caleb?"

Caleb nods again.

"We do that for Diwali too! One thing I love about Christmas, though, is the silly sweaters. Last year, my dad wore a sweater with Santa dabbing on it," Dev laughs. They giggle and dab along with Dev.

"I love that my house shimmers with lights from Diwali to New Year," Riya sighs and crosses her fingers. "I wish it snows and we have a white Christmas."

Dev adds, "I hope my Amamma and Thatha can visit during the festive season this year. It is so much more fun celebrating with the whole family.

My mom says Diwali is celebrated in South India because Lord Krishna defeated the demon king Narakasura, saving 16,000 women."

Riya lifts a finger and says, "My ma says Diwali is celebrated in North India because Lord Ram came home to Ayodhya after winning the war against the demon king of Lanka, Ravan.

Ma says people around the world celebrate Diwali for different reasons. Some people even call it Deepavali, meaning rows of lighted diyas or lamps."

"Interesting! Christmas is celebrated because Christ, the Son of God, was born and it was so wonderful that he came to earth. Mass is always so peaceful, " Ella shares.

"Each morning before Christmas,
I open a new window in the advent calendar.
The reindeer pictures are my favorite.

In the evenings, Mom and I bake different kinds
of cookies for the family and to share."

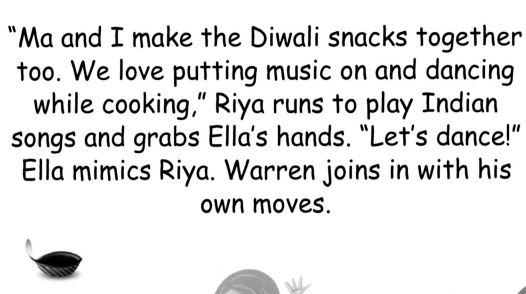

"Ma and I make the Diwali snacks together too. We love putting music on and dancing while cooking," Riya runs to play Indian songs and grabs Ella's hands. "Let's dance!" Ella mimics Riya. Warren joins in with his own moves.

Dev rolls his eyes and whispers to Caleb, "You don't have to if you don't want to. My mom keeps trying to get me to dance too, but I just like listening to Christmas carols when we put up our tree."

Riya stops dancing to sit with Dev and Caleb.
Riya says to Caleb, "Did you know different days
of Diwali have different rituals?" Caleb shakes his
head. Riya counts the 5 days of Diwali on her fingers.

3. Badi Diwali

4. Naya Saal

2. Choti Diwali

5. Bhaidooj

1. Dhanteras

Dev shrugs. "That's okay though. That's different everywhere too. In our home, we only celebrate it for two days. The best part of Diwali, though, has to be the firecrackers."

Caleb beams, "I love the firecrackers display on July 4th!"

Riya's dad enters the room with a box.
"That's great! Because it's time for firecrackers!"
He goes over the safety rules with them.
"Each one is equally important.",
he says.

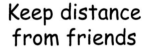

One at a time

Stay with adults

Keep distance
from friends

Keep a bucket of water close

Once done, clean up

They head out to play with sparklers, jumping up and down, squealing. Riya's dad sets the fireworks off. The dazzling lights and colors are amazing!

After they finish and go back inside, Warren asks Caleb, "Do you celebrate Diwali or Christmas?"

Caleb looks at them all and grins, "I'm Jewish. Hanukkah is our Festival of Lights. We light menorah for eight days with special prayers and enjoy fried foods.
The house sparkles in candlelight.
We also play dreidel games."

Riya claps her hands together, "That sounds wonderful! We can plan more festive playdates then."

Ella imagines making ornaments with her friends.
Warren talks about his grandma's fancy meals during Christmas.
Caleb can't wait to teach his new friends how to play dreidel.
Dev shares how they could also celebrate Holi when spring comes.

When it is time to leave, Riya gives them goody bags
full of Diwali snacks and the diyas they made.
They thank Riya and head home.
Their hearts glow with the joy of togetherness.
They wonder who else they could invite next time?

The End

# WHAT ARE OTHER ORIGINS OF DIWALI?

**Diwali is celebrated by people around the world for many different reasons.**

## Marwaris and Gujaratis

Merchants close the accounts of the old year and pray to Laxmi, the goddess of wealth, that the new year opens with even more success.

### Jainism

To the Jains, it marks the day after Lord Mahavira attained nirvana. He is said to be released from his worldly body on the night of the full moon, where he achieved nirvana (gained wisdom and was free of hatred and suffering). Lamps are lit in doorways as a symbol of this.

## Sikhism

For Sikhs, this day celebrates the release of Guru Hargobindji and 52 Indian kings imprisoned with him at the Gwalior fort in India by Emperor Shah Jahan in 1619. This day is also known as Bandi Chorr Diwas (meaning 'the day of freedom').

### Nepal

Diwali is also celebrated in Nepal and the Indian states of Assam, Sikkim, and Darjeeling in West Bengal. Their five-day festival is of great importance as it shows respect to humans and the Gods, but also to animals like crows, cows, and dogs.

## Historically

Diwali day is celebrated as the coronation of one of India's greatest kings, Vikramaditya. He was crowned on Diwali day, making it a historical event.

# WHY IS HANUKKAH CELEBRATED?

Approximately 2,200 years ago, there was a war between the Greeks and Jews. When the Greeks won, they forced their culture on the Jews. A group of Jewish people called the Maccabees fought back and freed Jerusalem. As part of the celebration, they needed to relight the menorah in their sacred temple.

The Jewish people found a single jar of oil, which would only last one day. They took a leap of faith and relit the menorah. To their surprise, the menorah stayed lit for eight days. It was a miracle! Hanukkah is eight-days long, celebrating each day the oil lasted. On each day, a branch of the nine-branch Hanukkah menorah is lit with the shamash (helper candle), which sits on the middle branch.

# ACTIVITY TIME

Making wheat flour diyas is a wonderfully eco-friendly way to celebrate. Just remember, you must make the diyas the day you want to use them. Adding oil to the dough helps them last about a week.

1. You need wheat flour (2 cups), water (¾ cup), oil (2-3 teaspoons), and a pinch of turmeric.
2. Knead the dough till its firm to the touch. Keep it aside to rest for 15-20 minutes.
3. Divide the dough into equal portions, making smooth balls.
4. Shape the diyas as you would like. There are many ways you can shape them – two examples are shown here.
5. Make a hole in the centre with your finger so we can add oil to light the diyas.
6. Pinch out some dough from the sides you want the wick to stick out from.
7. You can make designs on the diya with a pencil, fork, or butter knife.
8. Bake the diyas at 400 degrees for 45 minutes, or till they're hard to the touch.
9. Leave them out to cool.
10. Decorate the diyas with paint, glitter, small beads etc. as you like.

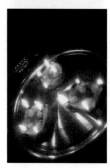

*I like to keep mine as is, because the glow of the diya is beautiful in itself.*

# CONVERSATION STARTERS

**Use the talking points below to build much needed conversation.**

- Caleb is new to the neighborhood, yet he came along. What do you think about that?
- What part of the story is your favorite? Why?
- What are some ways you can make friends part of your celebrations?
- What do you love most about the festivals you celebrate?
- What is the same and different about celebrations around the world?
- Have you tried any new foods lately?
- You read about Diwali, Hanukkah, and Christmas. What did you like the most about these festivals?
- What do you learn from the origin stories you read?
- If you could create a festival, what would it look like?

## How to Plan a Festival Themed Playdate

**Write down or draw your answers below to plan your very own festival playdate. Remember to keep things simple and keep in mind your guests while planning.**

- What celebration would you pick as the theme?
- Who will you invite?
- How will you decorate for the same?
- What will you wear?
- Think of crafts you can do and list supplies you will need.
- What food will you serve?
- What games will you play?

*Namaste. This is my second book in the Sparkling Me Empowerment Series. If you enjoyed this book, I'd appreciate it if you could leave a few encouraging words for me as a review on Amazon/ Goodreads, or on our website. Tag @raisingworldchildren whenever you share a picture.*

*Keep sparkling!*

## Aditi Wardhan Singh

Aditi Wardhan Singh is multi award-winning, bestselling author of books like 'Strong Roots Have No Fear' and 'How Our Skin Sparkles'. Featured on a number of global publications and broadcasts, she is one of the leading voices on cultural sensitivity and self-empowerment. In 2017, she founded RaisingWorldChildren. com, a global online and in print publication for multicultural families.

Aditi is an Indian American, raised in Kuwait. Her books aim to give children a strong sense of identity while building cultural awareness, with a sprinkle of faith and science. They're excellent resources for counselors, parents, and teachers for creating positive and impactful conversations. There are plenty of free articles, resources, and real stories of multicultural families on RaisingWorldChildren.com

**Connect with Aditi and find more multicultural reads here –**
Instagram - @raisingworldchildren
Facebook - @raisingworldchildren

**Also Available:**

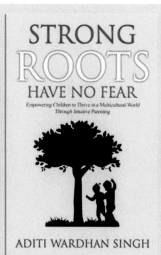
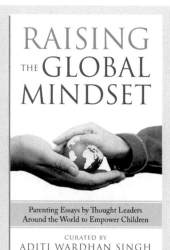

Made in the USA
Coppell, TX
21 February 2024

29267225R00021